A book about cuts, scratches, and scrapes

by Melvin Berger
Illustrated by Pat Stewart

Lodestar Books
Dutton · New York

Library of Congress Cataloging-in-Publication Data

Berger, Melvin.

Ouch!: a book about cuts, scratches, and scrapes/
by Melvin Berger: illustrated by Pat Stewart.—1st ed.
p. cm.
Summary: Describes in simple scientific detail how the body
heals itself when cuts, scratches, and scrapes occur.
ISBN 0-525-67323-7
1. Wounds and injuries—Juvenile literature. 2. Wound healing—
Juvenile literature. [1. Wounds and injuries. 2. Wound healing.]
I. Stewart, Pat Ronson, ill. II. Title.
RD93.B43 1991
617.1—dc20
90-34145 CIP AC

Published in the United States by Lodestar Books,
an affiliate of Dutton Children's Books,
a division of Penguin Books USA Inc.

Published simultaneously in Canada by
McClelland & Stewart, Toronto

Editor: Virginia Buckley Designer: Marilyn Granald, LMD

Printed in Hong Kong
First Edition 10 9 8 7 6 5 4 3 2 1

You break a glass and cut your finger. OUCH!
You climb a tree and scratch your arm. OUCH!
You fall down and scrape your knee. OUCH!

Cuts and scrapes happen to everyone. When they do, they hurt. OUCH! They also bleed. Bright red blood trickles out of the open wound.

Yet, it doesn't take very long for the cut or scrape to stop hurting. The blood dries up. After several days, the cut is healed.

How does your body stop the bleeding?

How does it heal the wound?

The answers may amaze you!

When you cut your skin, you also cut some of the blood vessels. Blood vessels are tubes that run through your skin and the rest of your body. All together your body contains about 100,000 miles of blood vessels! Blood is always flowing through them.

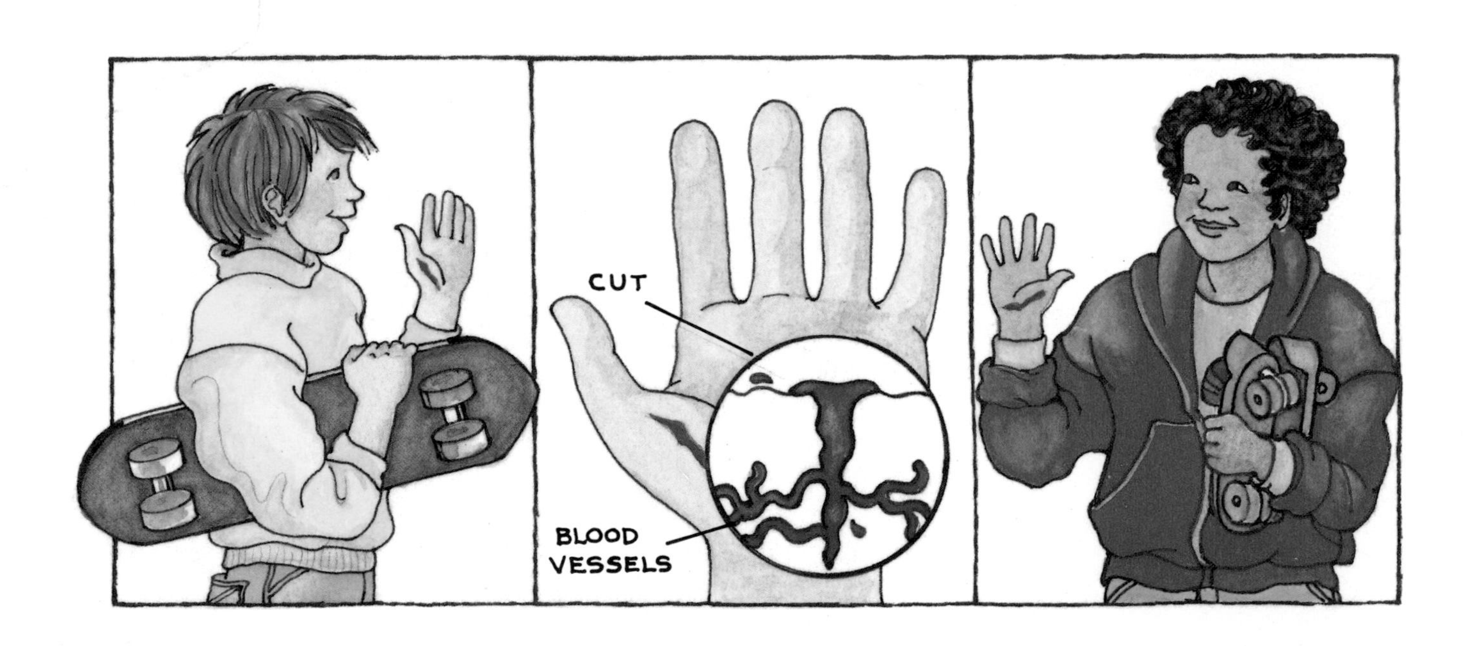

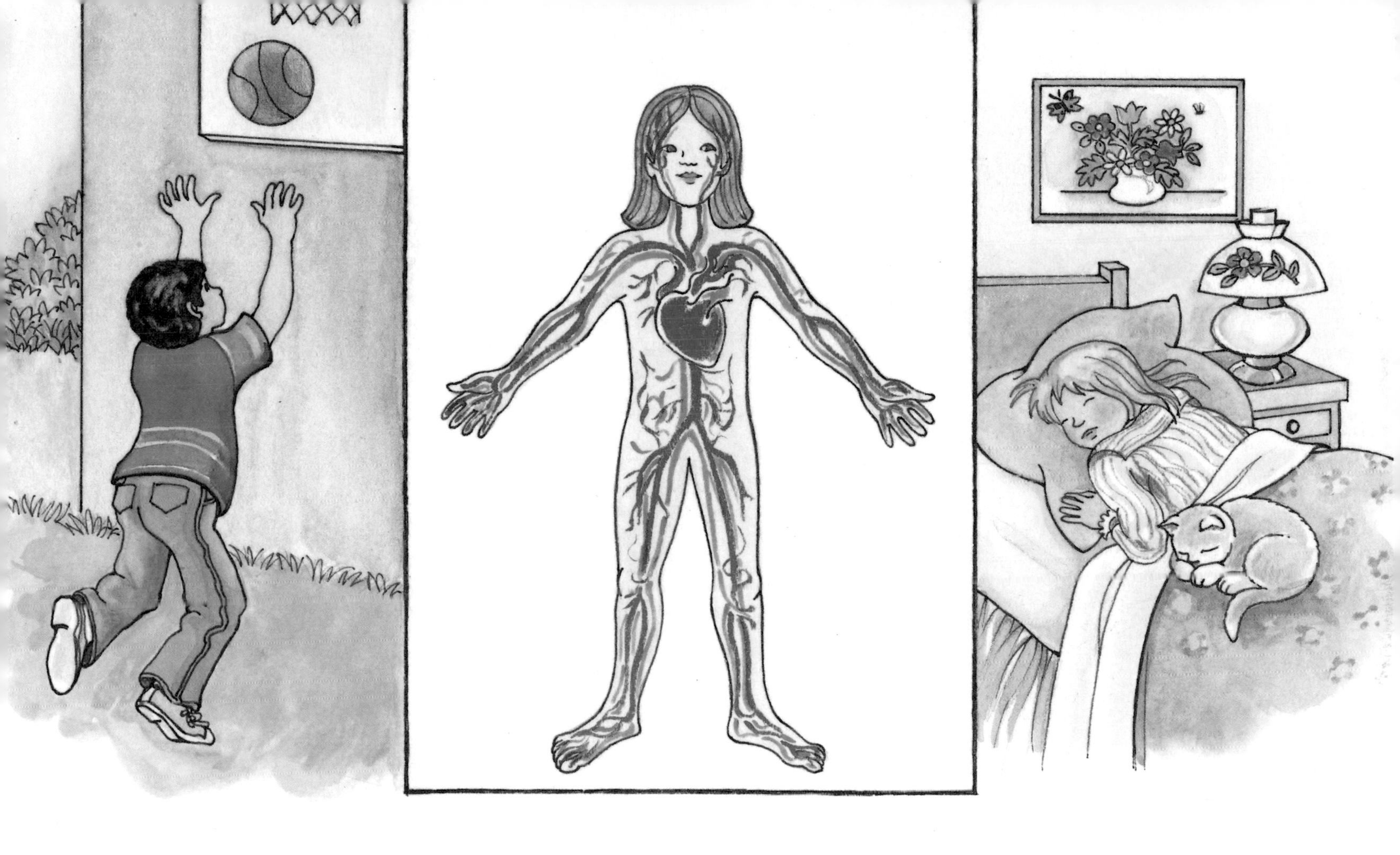

Day and night, whether you're asleep or awake, your heart is pumping blood through the blood vessels.

When you cut a blood vessel, blood leaks out. Don't get scared. Wash the cut right away and cover it with a Band-Aid. Now the blood can help mend the cut and heal the wound.

Here's how it works.

Let's say you pick up a piece of broken glass. OUCH! You've cut yourself. Your finger starts to bleed. Some blood is escaping through the break in the skin.

Blood is a liquid. But floating in the blood are tiny, solid bits of matter. These are called cells. Most are red blood cells. They give blood its rich, red color.

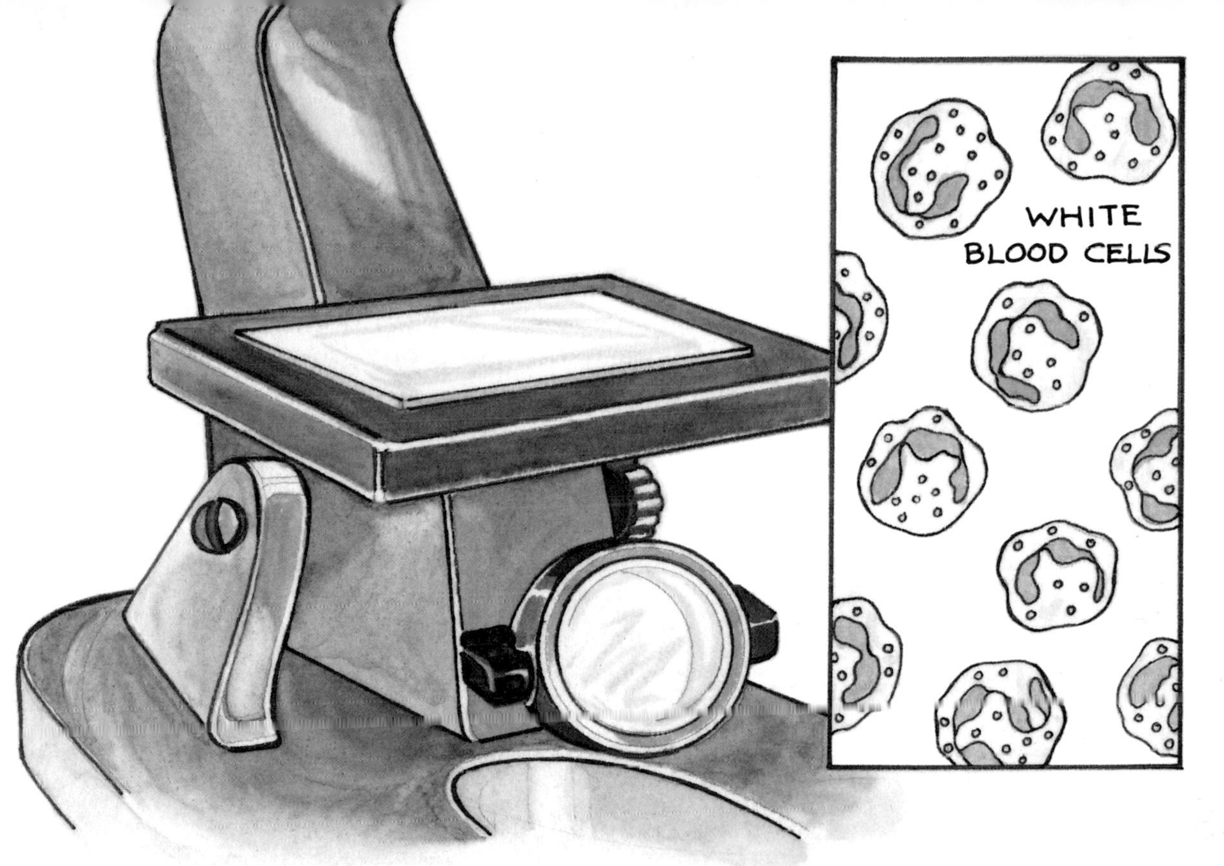

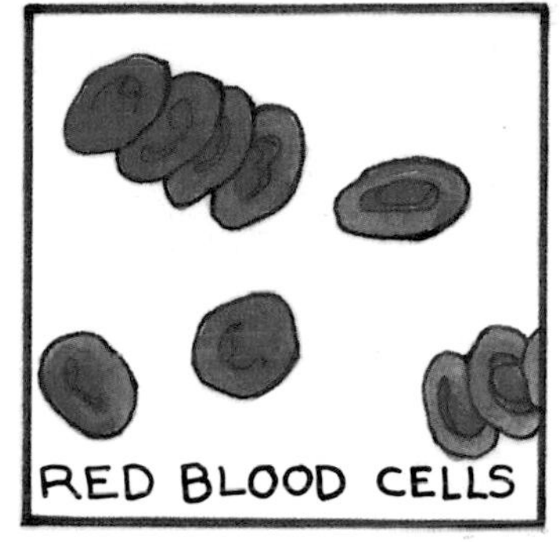

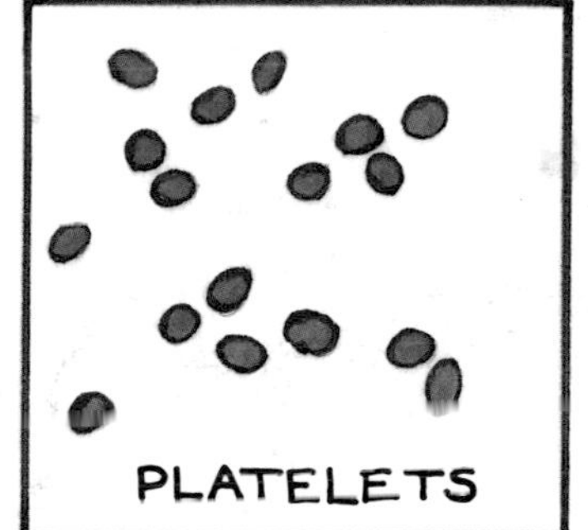

Some are white blood cells. The white blood cells are much larger than the red blood cells.

There are also platelets in the blood. They are called *plate*lets because they look like little round or oval plates. Platelets are very tiny bits of cells.

The cells and platelets are always being carried along in the blood. But when the platelets come to a cut, they get stuck. They cling to the break in the blood vessel.

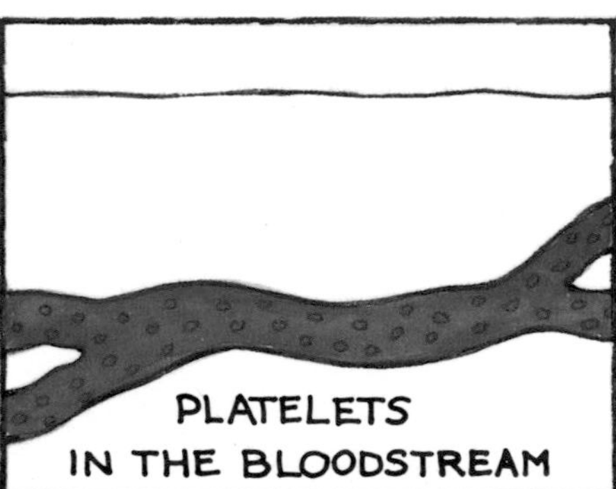

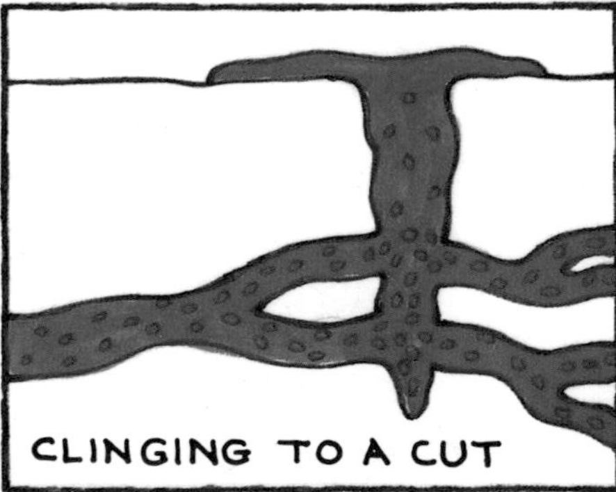

More and more platelets pile up around the cut. Soon there are so many of them that they plug up the break in the blood vessel. No more blood can flow out. Your cut stops bleeding.

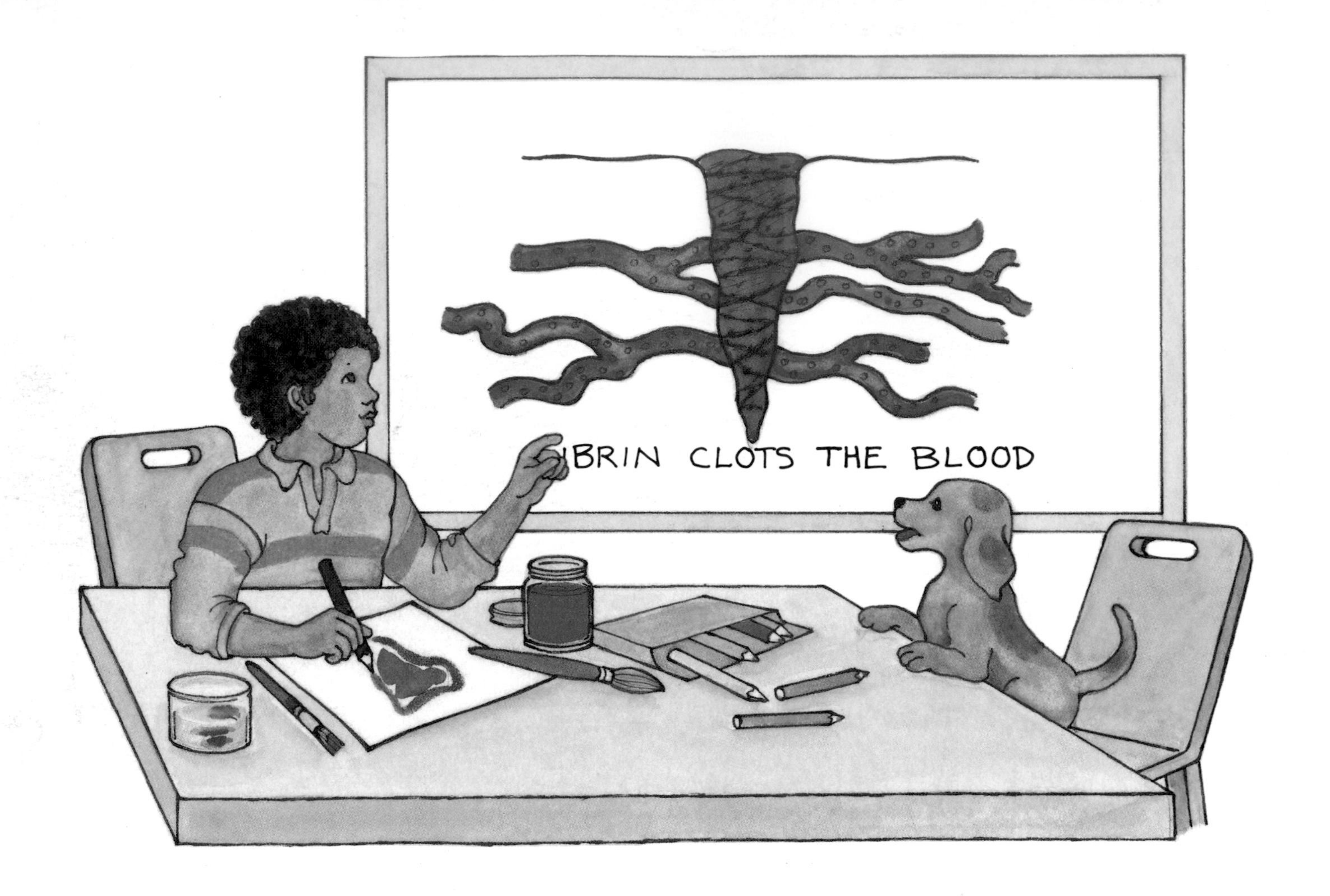

As the platelets crowd together, they give off a chemical. This chemical causes stiff, stringlike fibers called fibrin to form in the blood.

The threads of fibrin come together inside the cut. Up and down, side to side, backward and forward—they weave a net. This net holds the platelets and other blood cells in place.

After a while, the fibrin threads start to tighten. They pull all the cells and platelets closer together. The blood becomes thicker and thicker. Soon it is like jelly. Then we know that the blood has clotted.

An hour or two passes. The top part of the clotted blood becomes very dry. It forms a hard, brownish scab over the cut. The scab is like a shield. It protects the cut.

The scab keeps out germs. Germs, or bacteria, are tiny living beings that can harm you. But some bacteria are already inside the cut. They enter every time you cut yourself. And they grow and multiply inside the wound.

The bacteria can be very dangerous. They give off poisons. These poisons may cause infections. If your cut becomes infected, the skin around the wound turns red. It also feels hot. And it hurts.

But while the blood is clotting and the scab is forming, something incredible is happening inside the cut. Your body is working to get rid of the harmful bacteria.

It is the job of the white blood cells to kill off the bacteria. The white cells get into the clotted blood. They move toward the bacteria. Fingerlike shoots reach out and surround the bacteria. These "fingers" close up around them. The bacteria disappear inside the white blood cells! In a little while, the bacteria are dead.

The same thing is happening to the bits of dirt that are in the cut. The white blood cells gobble them up, too. Soon the cut is free of both bacteria and dirt.

Sometimes you see a thick, white liquid oozing out of a cut. “That’s pus,” someone tells you.

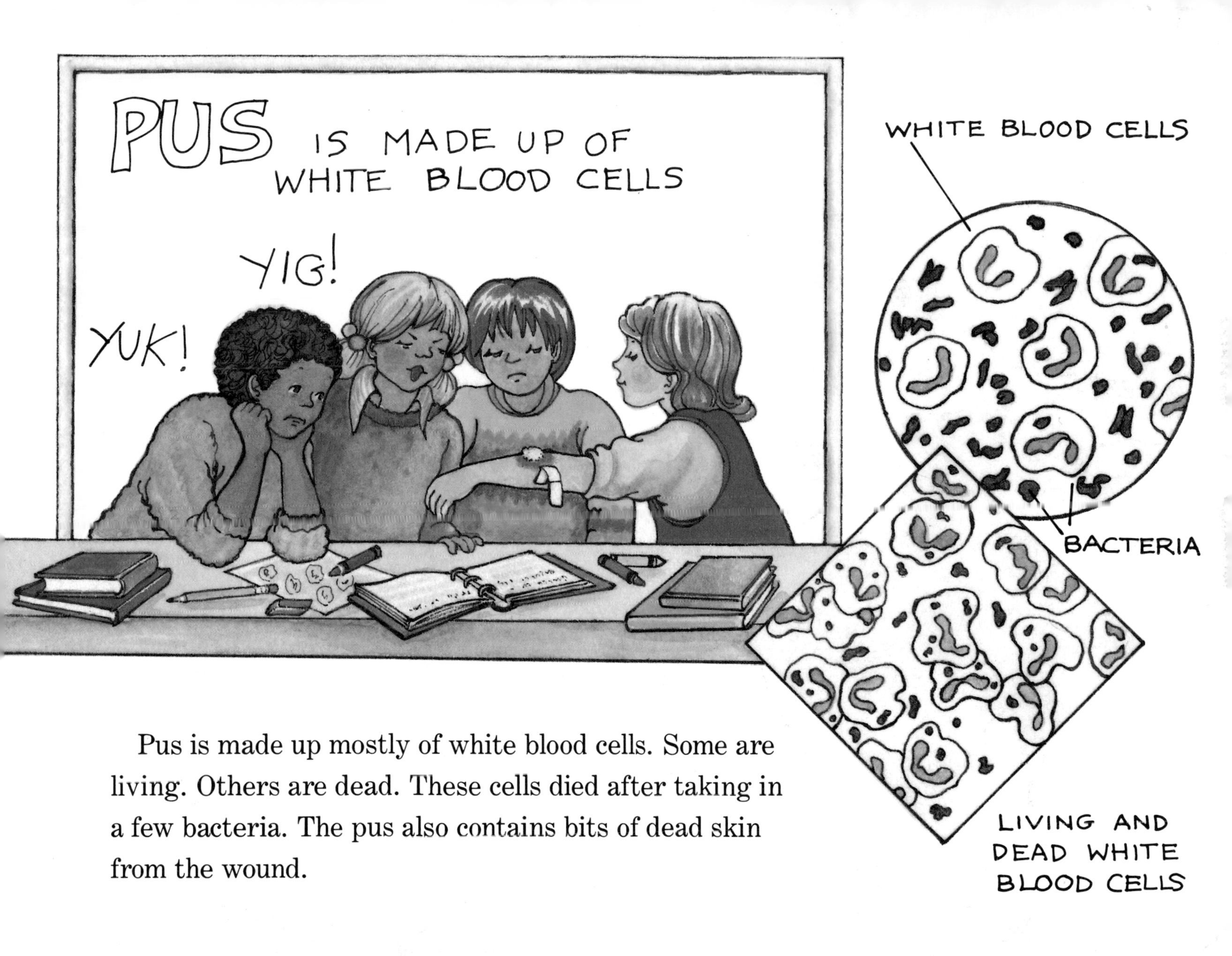

Pus is made up mostly of white blood cells. Some are living. Others are dead. These cells died after taking in a few bacteria. The pus also contains bits of dead skin from the wound.

So far the platelets and the fibrin have stopped the bleeding. The scab is keeping out more bacteria and dirt. And the white blood cells have cleaned out the wound.

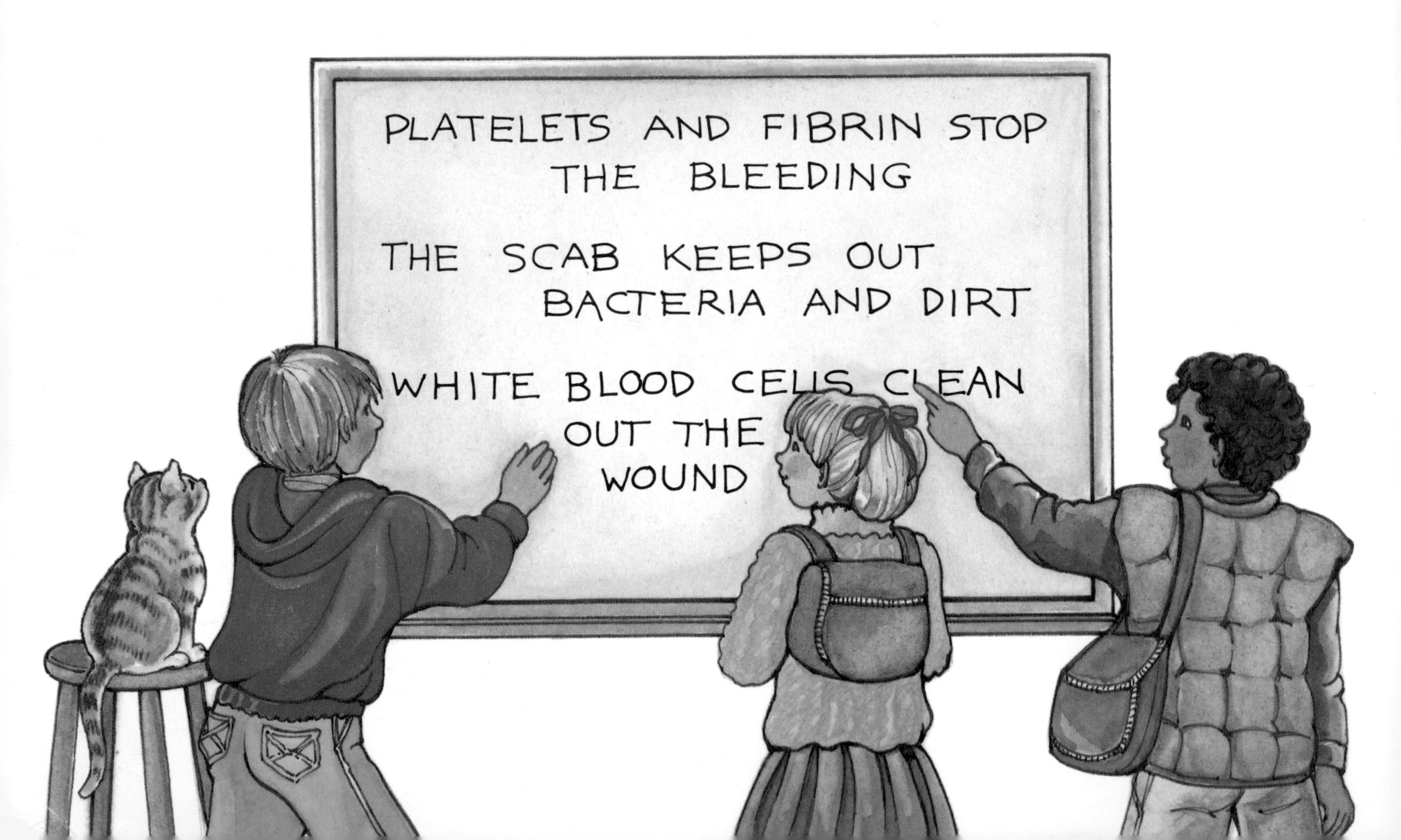

Now just one more thing must happen before you are completely healed. New skin must cover the cut.

Your skin is always growing. Old skin cells die. New skin cells take their place.

But the skin cells grow much faster around a cut. As the new skin cells form, they slide in under the scab. Soon the cells form a thin layer across the break in the skin.

Layers of skin build up. Finally the skin is so thick that the scab falls off.

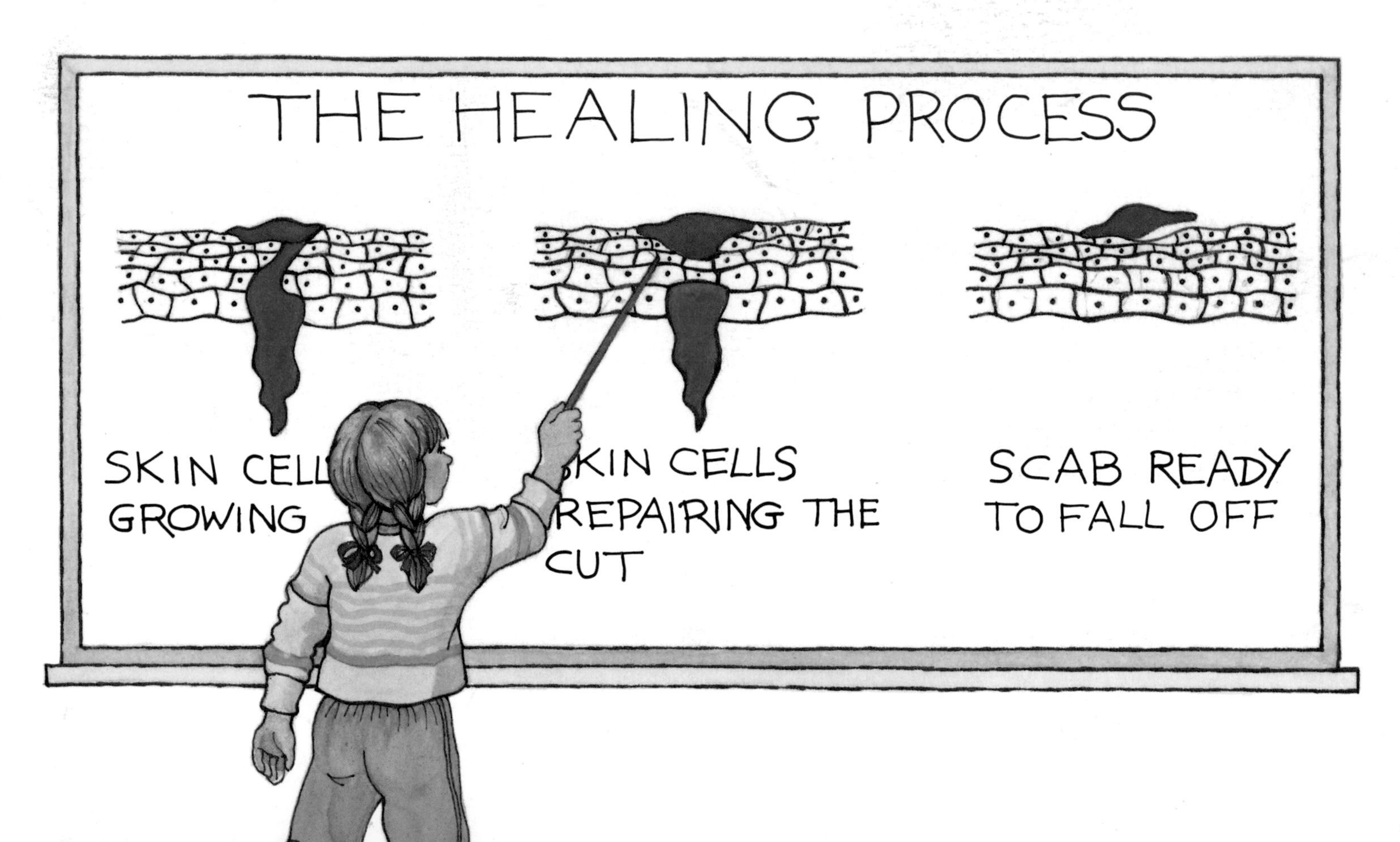

Picking at the scab slows down the healing process. It may also make the wound start to bleed again. More bacteria and dirt can get in. The cut could even get infected.

That's why you should always let the scab fall off by itself. In its place you'll see a pink line or circle. It marks the spot where you were cut. It looks pink because the skin there is still quite thin. You can actually see the blood vessels underneath.

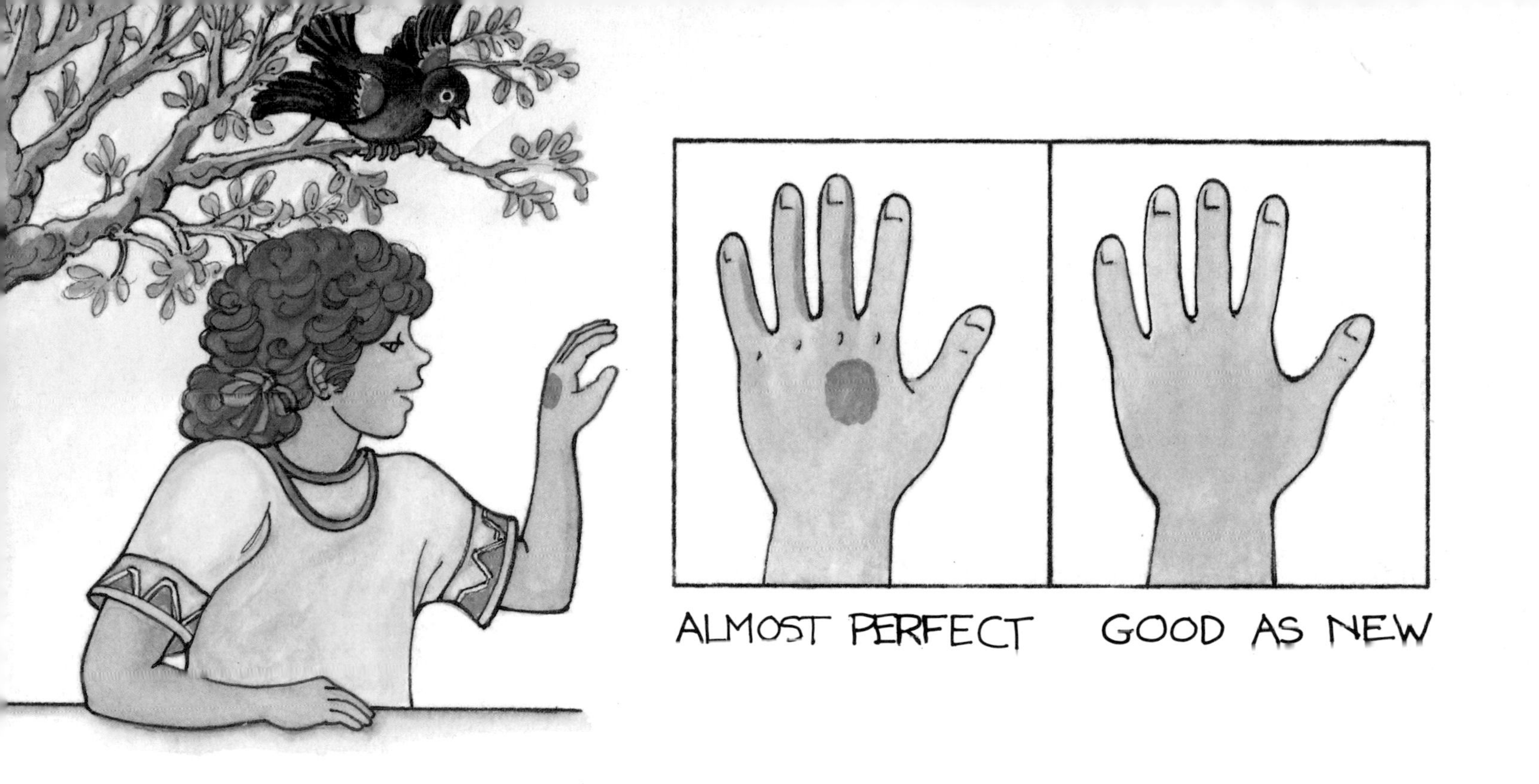

Soon the skin grows back to its full thickness. The pink mark disappears. The skin becomes the same color as the rest of your body. Sometimes it is even hard to remember where you cut yourself!

THIRD GRADE SCI
BACTERIA
ISN'T THIS GREAT?
PLATELETS STOP THE BLEEDING
FIBRIN CLOTS THE BLOOD
A SCAB FORMS ON TOP

NCE FAIR

Isn't it amazing how your body heals itself?

THINGS YOU SHOULD DO TO HELP

1 WASH THE WOUND

2 COVER IT WITH A BAND-AID

3 SEE A NURSE OR DOCTOR IF THE BLEEDING DOESN'T STOP

And before you know it—you're as good as new!